FRAIDY CATS

For my sisters and all the "S" cats
-S.K.

To Dundee and Bones
-B.L.

Library of Congress Cataloging-in-Publication Data

Krensky, Stephen, author.
Fraidy cats / by Stephen Krensky ; illustrated by Betsy Lewin. – (New edition).
pages cm. — (Scholastic reader. Level 2)
"Originally published: New York : Scholastic, 1993."
Summary: One dark and noisy night the Fraidy Cats let their imaginations run wild, visualizing scary things from wild elephants to hungry wolves.
ISBN 0-545-79966-X (pbk.) — ISBN 0-545-80160-5 (ebook) — ISBN 0-545-80161-3 (eba ebook)
1. Cats—Juvenile fiction. 2. Fear of the dark—Juvenile fiction. 3. Night—Juvenile fiction. 4. Bedtime—Juvenile fiction. 5. Stories in rhyme. (1. Stories in rhyme. 2. Cats—Fiction. 3. Fear of the dark—Fiction. 4. Night—Fiction. 5. Bedtime—Fiction.) I. Lewin, Betsy, illustrator. II. Title.
PZ8.3.K869Fr 2015
(E)—dc23
2014045467
CIP
AC

10 9 8 7 6 5 4 3 2 1 15 16 17 18 19/0

Printed in the U.S.A. 40
This edition first printing, September 2015
Book design by Maria Mercado

FRAIDY CATS

by Stephen Krensky
Illustrated by Betsy Lewin

SCHOLASTIC INC.

One dark night
when the wind blew hard,
the Fraidy Cats got ready for bed.
Scamper checked in the closet.
Nothing was there.
Sorry checked under the beds.
Nothing there, either.

They checked behind the curtains
and the door.
All was well.
They crawled into their beds
and fixed the covers.
"Good night," said Scamper.
"Pleasant dreams," said Sorry.
Then they heard a noise.

TAP, TAP, TAP!

"I hear a dog," said Sorry.

"A big hairy dog."

"Is it friendly?" Scamper asked.

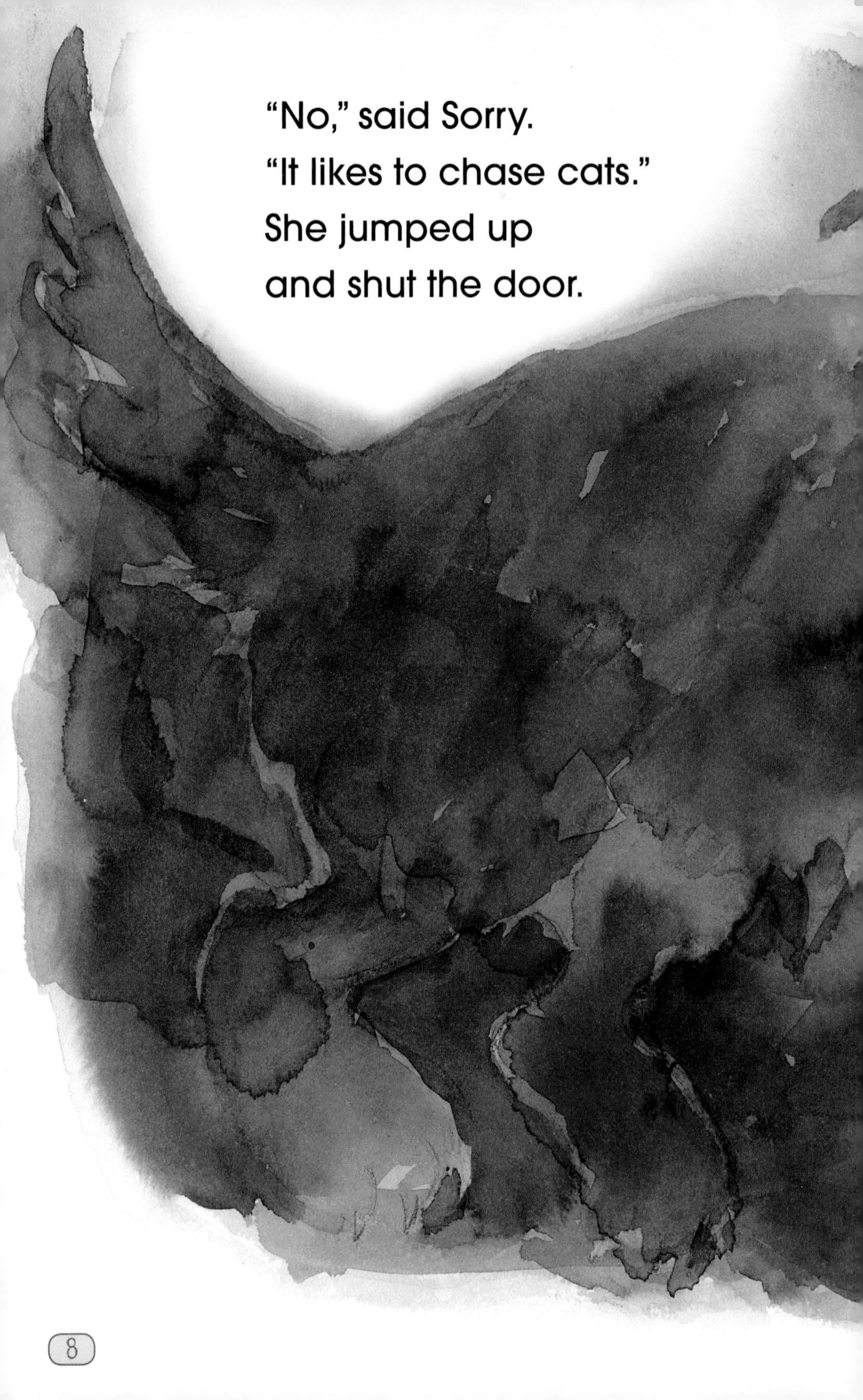

"No," said Sorry.
"It likes to chase cats."
She jumped up
and shut the door.

HISSSSS!

“I hear a snake,” said Scamper.

“It scared the dog away.”

“Is it a cute little garden snake?”

Sorry asked.

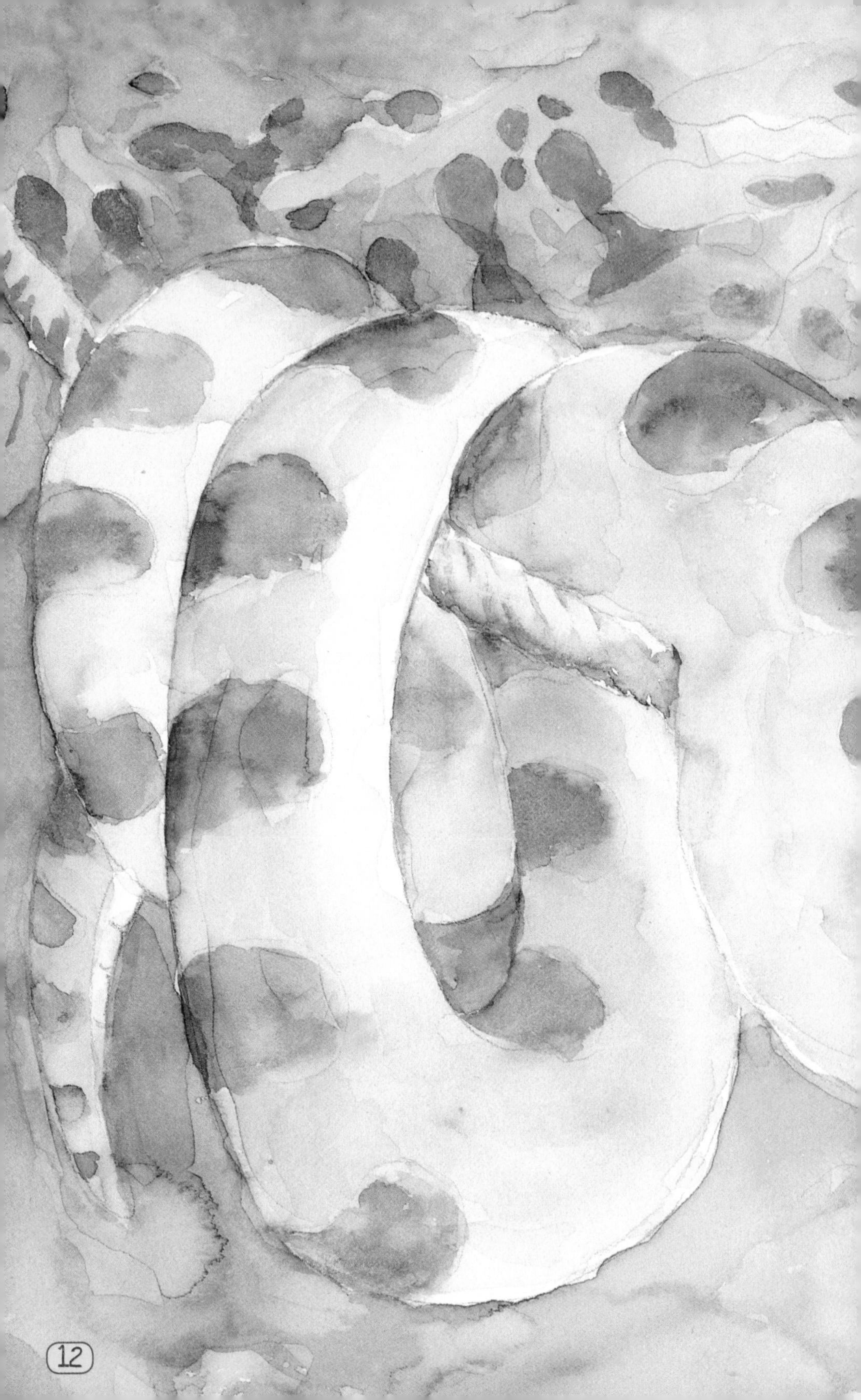

"No," said Scamper.
"It's a long giant snake—and
it hasn't eaten in a week."
He got up
and pushed a blanket
in the crack under the door.

SCREECH!

"I hear an eagle," said Sorry.

"It scared the snake away."

"Is it a gentle baby eagle?"

asked Scamper.

Sorry shook her head.
"It's a fierce mountain eagle,
swooping down from the clouds
to carry something back
to its rocky nest."
She ran to the window
and shut it.

WOOO! WOOO!

"I hear a wolf," said Scamper.

"It scared the eagle away."

"Is this a wolf that only likes to eat three little pigs?" asked Sorry.

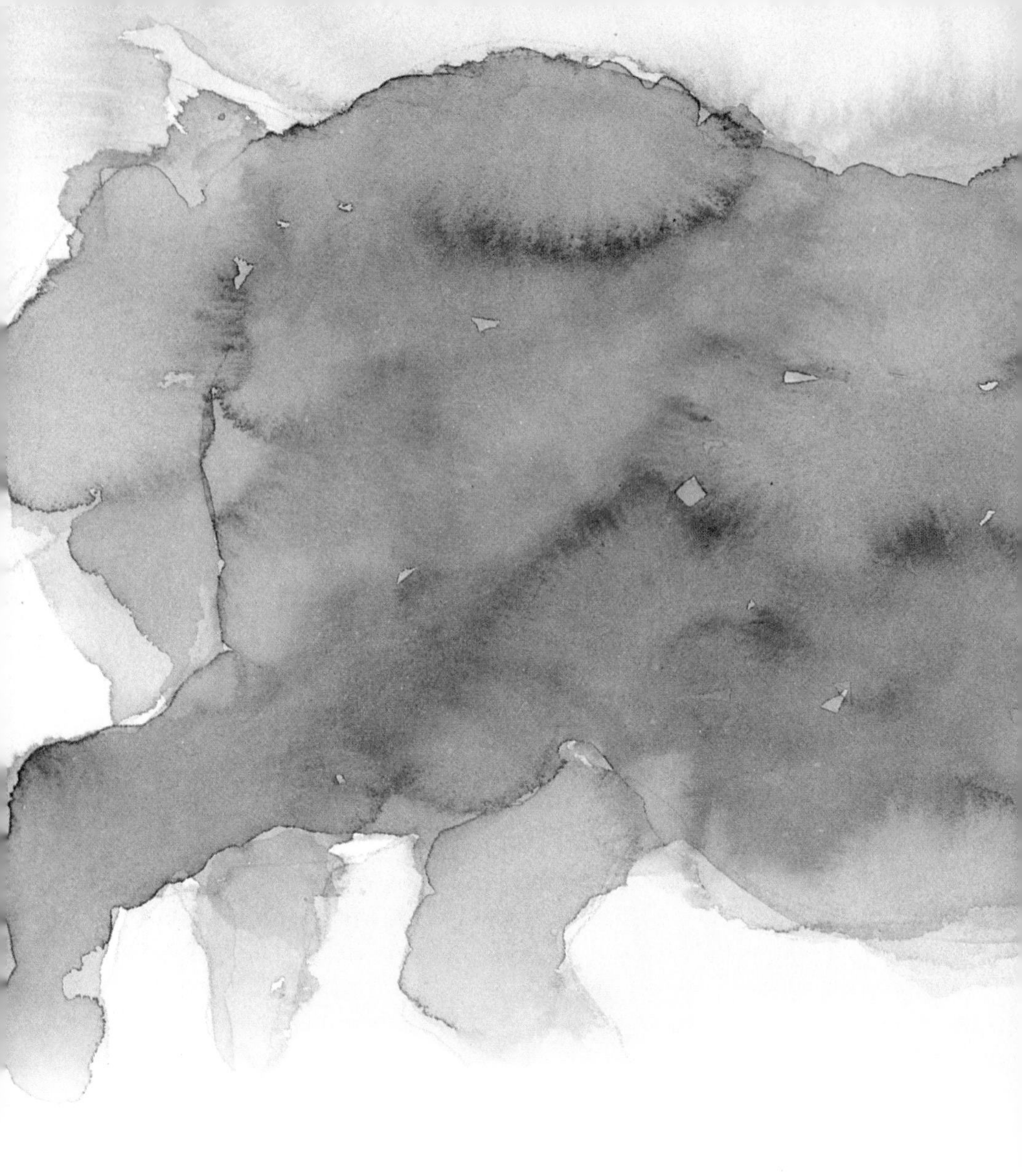

“Oh no,” said Scamper.
“This is a wolf
with many sharp teeth.
It will eat almost anything it sees.”
He ran to the window
and shut the curtains.

ROOOORRR!

“I hear an elephant,” said Sorry.

“It scared the wolf away.”

“Is this a tame elephant
that ran away from the circus?”
Scamper asked.

“No,” said Sorry.
“This is a wild elephant
with legs like tree trunks.
It crushes things that get in its way.”
Scamper and Sorry
looked at each other
and dove under their beds.

BOOM! BOOM!

"I hear a dinosaur," said Scamper.

"It scared the elephant away."

"Is this a small dinosaur

the size of a lizard?" Sorry asked.

Scamper bit his lip.

"It is as big as a house," he said.

"And there's nothing left to close
or lock or hide under.
We can't stop it."
Sorry poked her head out.
"Wait a minute," she said.
"What kind of dinosaur is it?"
Scamper wasn't sure.

BOOM! BOOM! BOOM!

The room shook.

The windows rattled.

"It must be a tremendosaurus.

The biggest, heaviest dinosaur

that ever lived.

We're doomed," said Sorry.

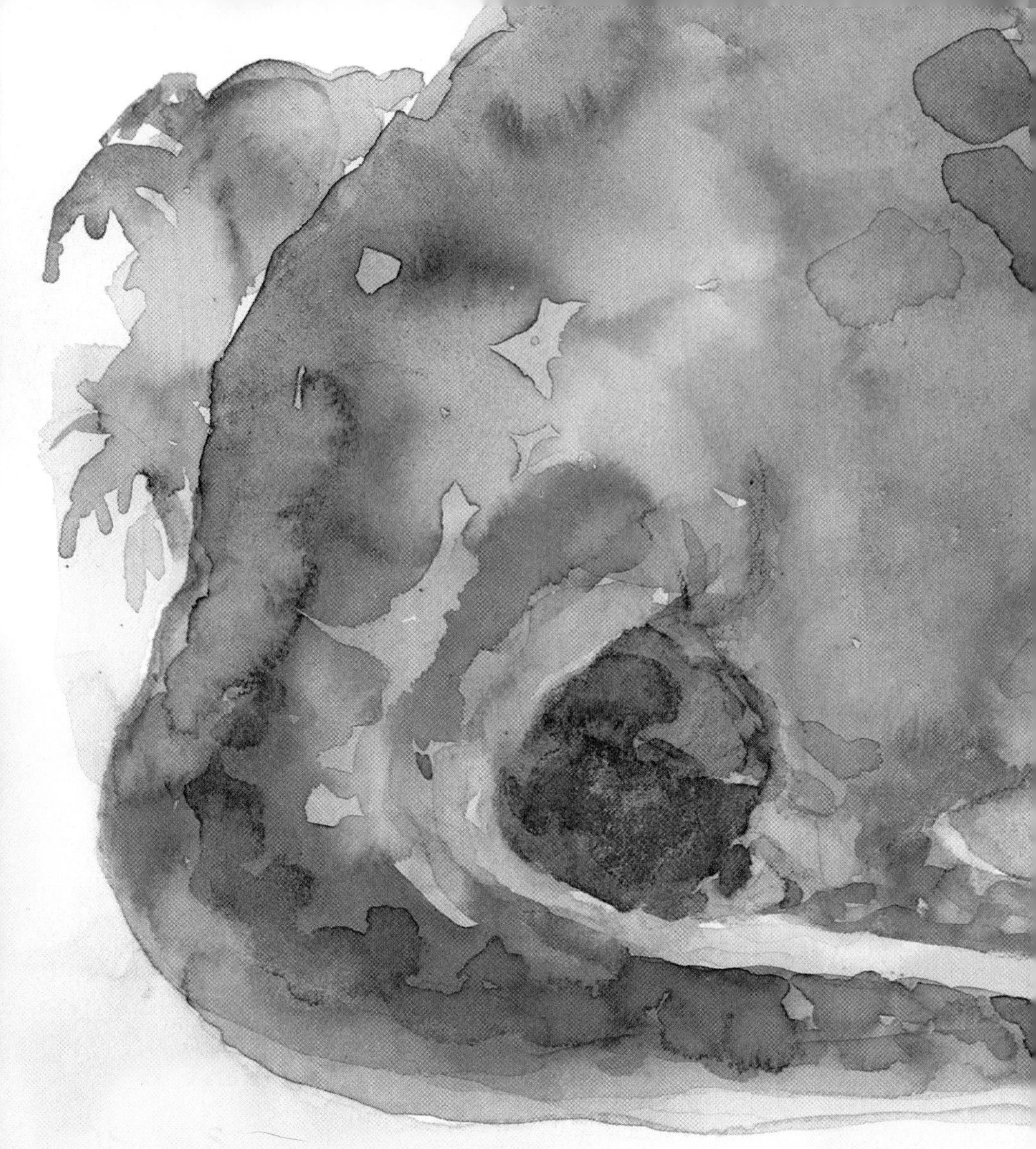

Scamper frowned.
"Wait a minute. I've read about tremendosaurs. They only ate plants."
"Are you sure?"
"Positive."
"No cats?"
Scamper shook his head.

Sorry smiled.
"Then the tremendosaurus
will stay in the garden," she said.
"And, it will scare away anything
else that comes by," said Scamper.
"We're safe at last."

The night was still dark.
The wind still blew hard.
But the Fraidy Cats didn't care.
They got back into bed
and fixed the covers.
"Good night!" they said together,
and then fell fast asleep.